Isabelle Harper

OUR
NEW PUPPY

Illustrated by Barry Moser

THE BLUE SKY PRESS
An Imprint of Scholastic Inc. • *New York*

THE BLUE SKY PRESS

For information regarding permission, please write to:
Permissions Department,
The Blue Sky Press, an imprint of Scholastic Inc.,
555 Broadway, New York, New York 10012.
The Blue Sky Press is a registered trademark of Scholastic Inc.
Library of Congress Cataloging-in-Publication Data
Harper, Isabelle.
Our new puppy / Isabelle Harper; illustrated by Barry Moser.
p.   cm.
Summary: When the puppy Floyd joins the family, Eliza and
Isabelle see how Rosie the family dog reacts and learn
what it is like having and being a younger sibling.
ISBN 0-590-56926-0
[1. Dogs — Fiction.]   I. Moser, Barry, ill.   II. Title.
PZ7.H23133Ou   1996   [E] — dc20   95-26168   CIP   AC
12 11 10 9 8 7 6 5 4 3 2 1   6 7 8 9/9 0 1/0
Printed in Singapore   46
First printing, September 1996
The illustrations in this book were executed with watercolor on paper
handmade by Simon Green at the Barcham Green Mills in Maidstone,
Kent, Great Britain, especially for the Royal Watercolor Society.
Production supervision by Angela Biola
Art direction by Kathleen Westray
Designed by Barry Moser

For the dogs whose devotion and companionship
have, over the years, enriched our lives:
Pinocchio and Penny, Boots and Lady, Cleo and Emily,
Hansel and Gretel, O.B., Abigail, Lord Jeffrey Amherst,
and especially to Floyd and Rosie's
dearly departed housemate and friend,
Woody Wilson.

"OUR NEW PUPPY, Floyd, is coming to live with us tomorrow," Grandpa tells Eliza and Isabelle.

"Will Rosie like Floyd?" Eliza wants to know.

"Probably not at first," Grandpa says. "But someday he will."

The next day, Aunt Maddy drives up with a big basket in her car.

"Look, Grandpa," Isabelle says. "It's Floyd!"

Sure enough, there he is.

"Grandpa," Eliza says, "I didn't know Floyd would be this little."

"Yes," Grandpa says, "Floyd is much smaller than Rosie.
He's only eight weeks old."

"Is Floyd a baby?" Eliza wants to know.
"Yes," Grandpa tells her. "He's a baby dog."

From the start, Floyd loves Rosie.
He follows Rosie everywhere he goes.
At first, Rosie's not sure what to do.

Floyd tries to play with Rosie.

He chews on Rosie's ears.

When Rosie isn't looking, Floyd steals his favorite toys . . .

and tears them up.

When nobody's watching,
Floyd eats some of Rosie's snack.

And in the afternoon, Rosie's friend Oscar comes to visit. But this time, Oscar doesn't stay long.

At first, Rosie wasn't sure if he would like
the new puppy. But soon, he likes the company.
Especially when Floyd's asleep.

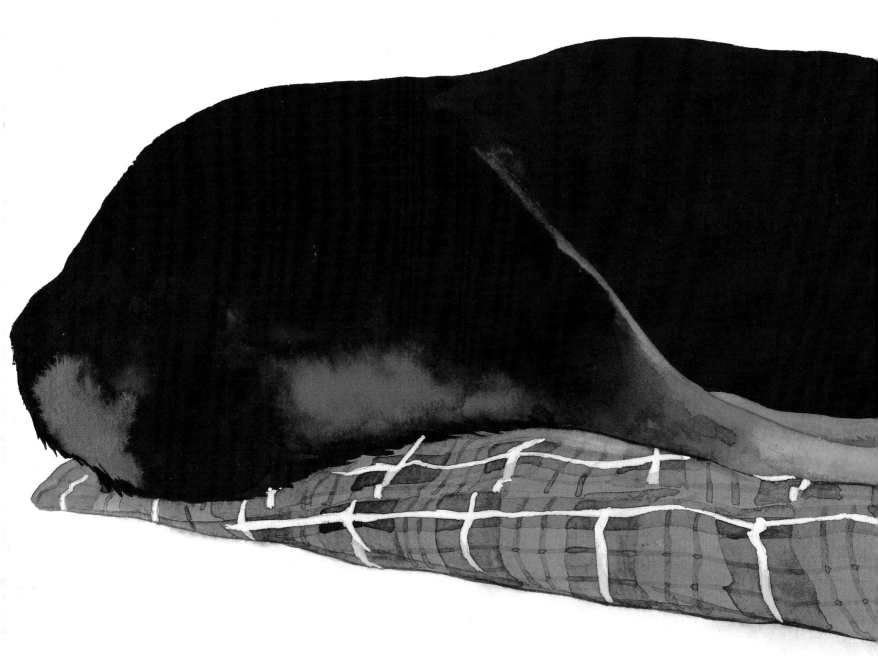

"I wasn't sure I wanted a baby sister either,"
Isabelle tells Eliza. "But now I do."

"Floyd loves Rosie," Eliza says. "And I love you."